Copyright © 1999 by Nord-Süd Verlag AG, Gossau Zürich, Switzerland
First published in Switzerland under the title *Peter und der Wolf*
English translation copyright © 1999 by North-South Books Inc.

First published in the United States, Great Britain, Canada,
Australia, and New Zealand in 1999 by North-South Books,
an imprint of Nord-Süd Verlag AG, Gossau Zürich, Switzerland.
Distributed in the United States by North-South Books Inc., New York.

Library of Congress Cataloging-in-Publication Data is available.
A CIP catalogue record for this book is available from The British Library.

ISBN 0-7358-1188-1 (TRADE BINDING)
1 3 5 7 9 TB 10 8 6 4 2
ISBN 0-7358-1189-X (LIBRARY BINDING)
1 3 5 7 9 LB 10 8 6 4 2
Printed in Belgium

For more information about our books,
and the authors and artists who create them,
visit our web site: http://www.northsouth.com

PETER
AND THE WOLF

BY SERGEI PROKOFIEV · ILLUSTRATED BY JULIA GUKOVA

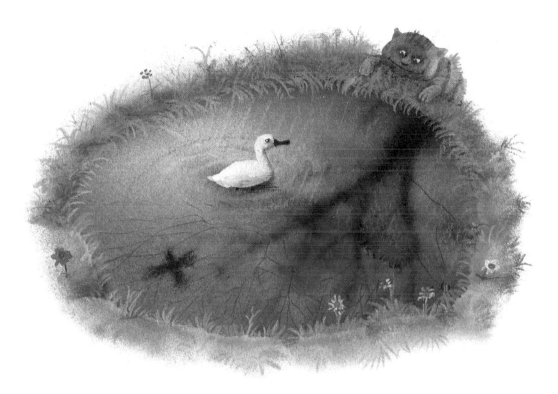

ADAPTED BY GERLINDE WIENCIRZ
TRANSLATED BY ANTHEA BELL

NORTH-SOUTH BOOKS

NEW YORK · LONDON

THE GREAT FOREST began just outside town, and in the forest there was a beautiful meadow with a little pond in it. An apple tree where a little bird had built its nest grew on the bank of the pond. One of the tree's sturdy branches hung above the fence and over a garden.

The duck lived in that garden.

There was a wooden house in the garden too, and Peter and his grandfather lived in the house. As for the old tabby cat, she was at home everywhere—in the garden, in the meadow, even in the forest.

One morning Peter woke up early. He went out into the garden
and looked around. Where was his friend the little bird? Peter gave
a soft whistle.

Another whistle answered him from the top of a tall tree, and the
little bird came flying down. He perched on Peter's hand, chirped,
and then flew away across the meadow.

"Catch me if you can!" called the bird. "Catch me if you can!"

Peter ran to the gate and threw it open. "Just you wait!" he
shouted as he ran through the grass, which was still wet with dew.
"I really will catch you one day!"

Wondering what was going on, the duck put her head around the open gate and looked at the pond.

"I think I'd like a nice bath!" she said to herself, and she waddled off.

"What a funny bird you are, dear duck!" the little bird mocked her. "You don't fly!" He took off into the air and came down again close to the duck, fluttering around her bill.

The duck took no notice. She just stretched her neck and quacked, "What a funny bird *you* are! You don't swim!"

She nibbled a clover leaf here and a flower there, and waddled on in the direction of the pond.

The cat stretched in the morning sunlight. When she heard the two birds arguing, she thought, This is my chance to catch them! Crawling through the grass and keeping low, she prowled closer and closer, paw by paw. Her whiskers were quivering with excitement.

But Peter had seen the cat and guessed her plan. "Watch out!" he shouted. "Watch out for the cat!"

Whoosh—the bird flew up into the tree!

Splash—the duck jumped into the water!

Oh, well, better luck next time, thought the cat, stretching out in the sun again.

Grandfather came into the garden. When he saw the open gate, he was angry.

"Peter, you know the wolf lives in the forest!" he said. "And you know how dangerous the wolf is. You mustn't leave the garden gate open!"

"But I've never seen the wolf, Grandfather," said Peter. "Anyway, I'm not afraid of him!"

"Then you ought to be," said Grandfather. "Now, come along and have your breakfast."

He took Peter by the arm and led him home, carefully closing the garden gate behind them.

No sooner had Peter and Grandfather disappeared into the house than the wolf came out of the forest. He had not eaten for a long time and he was hungry.

He saw the little bird, the old tabby cat, and the fat duck, and he raced toward them.

But the animals had seen him too. The bird flew higher up the tree, and the cat took a great leap and climbed its trunk.

In terror, the duck tried to save herself by jumping out of the pond and flying up into the tree too. But the wolf was too fast for her. He caught her—and swallowed her in one gulp.

But he was still hungry. Could he catch the other two? That would make a really good meal!

Peter, standing at the window, had seen it all. Grandfather was right: the wolf really was dangerous. But he had to warn his friends! He raced outside, stopping only to pick up a rope that was lying in the wheelbarrow.

First he climbed the fence. Then he cautiously made his way along the overhanging branch, inching slowly forward.

Now he could see the wolf jumping up at the tree again and again with his claws outstretched, trying to catch the cat.

"Little bird, you must lure the wolf away," whispered Peter. "But be careful he doesn't catch you!"

"Easy!" twittered the bird. He left his branch and flew in circles around the wolf's head, keeping as close as he dared. Peter quickly tied a loop in the end of the rope to make a lasso.

The wolf looked greedily at the bird. How he wanted to catch it! He only had to keep his eye on it . . .

The bird flew in circles closer and closer to the wolf's head, and the wolf turned around faster and faster to catch the bird, until at last he was giddy.

The wolf stopped. He was so dizzy. He shook himself. Seizing his chance, Peter threw his lasso over the wolf's head.

The wolf howled with rage and struggled to get free, running back and forth and racing around the tree. But the more he raged and the faster he ran, the tighter the rope became, until at last its whole length was wrapped around the tree. The wolf could go neither forward nor back.

"Caught you!" shouted Peter in delight. He jumped down from the fence and danced around the wolf.

The bird fluttered up on his shoulder.

"Caught him, caught him!" twittered the bird.

And the cat too mewed, "Caught him!" jumping up and down behind Peter.

Just then three hunters came out of the forest in a hurry. They were out of breath.

"We've caught that wicked wolf at last!" cried the first hunter, loading his rifle.

"No!" said Peter. "The bird and I caught him! You mustn't shoot him."

"Move aside! We're going to fire!" said the second hunter, aiming his gun.

BANG! The gun fired a shot, but in all the confusion it went up in the air and did no harm. The noise brought Grandfather out of the house.

"You can't shoot a captured animal!" said Grandfather indignantly, and he took the rifles away from the surprised hunters.

"Then what do we do with him?" asked the third hunter, pointing to the wolf.

"I know, Grandfather! Let's take him to the zoo!" suggested Peter.

"That's a good idea," said Grandfather. "But how?"

Peter went into the garden and came back with the wheelbarrow. Working together, they soon had the wolf securely tied up.

"Oh, well, maybe it's not such a bad notion," the hunters grudgingly admitted.

So they all set off for town. Peter went ahead with the little bird. Then came Grandfather, pushing the wheelbarrow with the wolf in it, and the hunters brought up the rear.

As for the old tabby cat, she wound around Peter's legs, and every now and then looked up at the bird and mewed her thanks.